WITHDRAWN

Goodnight,
Baby Flurry Heart

By Michael Vogel

Illustrated by Amy Mebberson

ORCHARD

Once upon a time, in the magical land of Equestria...

Two princesses stood high in a tower. Princess Celestia used her magic to lower the sun, while her sister, Princess Luna, used her magic to raise the moon. This let ponies across the land know it was time to sleep.

In the Crystal Empire, the Crystal Ponies saw the night sky and thanked Luna. Everypony was ready to get some good rest!

Well, *almost* everypony.

The royal baby, Princess Flurry Heart, was wide awake. In fact, Princess Cadance and Prince Shining Armor's daughter was not interested in going to sleep – at all.

Prince Shining Armor was at his wit's end.
Telling soldiers what to do was easier than
telling his daughter to go to sleep!

He tried giving her her favourite stuffed animal.

He tried singing a lullaby.

He even tried performing silly tricks.

But nothing worked! Flurry Heart just would not go to sleep.

Prince Shining Armor had one last idea.
He would tell Flurry Heart a bedtime story.
One that was exciting and daring and
full of adventure!

He tucked Flurry Heart into her crib
and started his story the way all
good bedtime stories do:

Once upon a time...

...there lived a brave and daring young unicorn who travelled across Equestria in search of adventure. Although he had battled timberwolves and cragadiles, he craved yet more excitement.

One day, the unicorn was travelling through the mysterious Everfree Forest when he came across a giant beanstalk growing high into the sky.

"Aha!" said the unicorn. "I bet there's a truly epic adventure at the top of this beanstalk. I'm going to climb it!"

And so he did.

When he reached the top, he found a giant castle. The unicorn watched as a giant pony peered out of a window at Equestria far, far below.

"Soon I will climb down my beanstalk and steal the land from all the little ponies. I will take their gems and force them to make me dinner!" shouted the giant pony. The unicorn knew he needed to save Equestria!

But just then the giant sniffed the air and bellowed–

"Um, sweetie, what are you doing?"

Prince Shining Armor turned to see Princess Cadance entering Flurry Heart's nursery. "I'm telling our daughter an exciting bedtime story, full of adventure, to get her to fall asleep!" he announced proudly.

Princess Cadance looked down at their baby, who was staring wide-eyed at her father. "I love you, sweetheart, but you don't know the first thing about a good bedtime story for a baby princess."

"You think you can do better?" Shining Armor asked.

"I was Princess Twilight's foal-sitter," said Cadance.
"I told her more bedtime stories than I can count!
Step aside and let a pro show you how it's done...

"Flurry Heart's bedtime story should be sweet and delightful and musical!"

She tucked Flurry Heart into her crib and started her story the way all good bedtime stories do:

Once upon a time...

...there was a young Alicorn princess who lived near the magical Everfree Forest. Everypony loved her because she had a beautiful singing voice and brought joy wherever she went. One day, the young princess wandered deep into the forest and lost her way...

But before she could get too scared, seven little dragons came out of the shadows and asked if they could help her.

The princess explained that she needed to find her way back to her castle. The dragons were happy to help, but they asked the princess if she would sing for them first.

♪!

And so she did.

The dragons were so happy that the princess had sung for them that they gave her the gems they were planning to eat for dinner.

The princess said she couldn't possibly take the gems, but the dragons said—

"A pro, huh? Just take a look at your daughter, foal-sitter extraordinaire."

Princess Cadance stopped her story and turned to look at Baby Flurry Heart. She wasn't in her crib! She had escaped across the nursery and was in the corner playing with her toys.

"You may have been good at telling bedtime stories to Twily," the prince said, "but our daughter felt your story was a little … *dull.*"

"Your story had timberwolves and cragadiles!" Princess Cadance argued. "It would have kept her up all night!"

Prince Shining Armor sighed. "Well, if my exciting story doesn't work and your sweet story doesn't work, how are we going to persuade Flurry Heart to go to sleep?"

Princess Cadance had an idea. "What if we tell a story ... *together*?"

"You mean a delightful adventure?" Prince Shining Armor asked.

"Something exciting *and* musical!" replied Princess Cadance.

They grinned at each other. "Daring *and* sweet!" they said at the same time.

And so Princess Cadance and Prince Shining Armor both tucked Flurry Heart into bed. And this time, they both began the story the way all good bedtime stories do:

...a dashing and daring unicorn was travelling through the mystical and mysterious Everfree Forest in search of adventure when he was stopped by seven little dragons. Their friend, a beautiful Alicorn princess, had been ponynapped by a giant pony! He had heard her beautiful songs, locked her in a cage in his castle, and forced her to sing for him!

The unicorn agreed to help the dragons. They took him through the forest to a clearing where a giant beanstalk grew high into the sky. They told him he would have to climb it to find the princess.

And so he did.

The unicorn climbed until he reached the giant pony's castle. He sneaked inside and found the princess. She was singing a sad, sad song. He told her not to worry - he was there to rescue her! The princess was delighted and told him that the key to her cage was on a chain around the giant's neck.

That night, the unicorn waited for the giant to fall asleep. Then he very carefully slipped the key from the giant's neck and used it to free the princess!

They were about to escape when the giant woke up!

"FEE-FI-FONEY-BALONEY! YOU TOOK MY KEY, YOU MISCHIEVOUS PONY!"

"Don't worry," said the princess. "I have an idea. We just need to–"

"Shhhhh, honey, look!"

Prince Shining Armor and
Princess Cadance looked into
the crib. Princess Flurry Heart
was fast asleep!

Princess Cadance slowly covered Flurry Heart with a blanket. Prince Shining Armor carefully arranged her favourite toys around her. They both crept quietly out of the nursery and Prince Shining Armor gently shut the door.

Prince Shining Armor turned to see Princess Cadance looking at him. "Well?" she asked.

"Well, what? We got Flurry Heart to go to sleep!"

"But we didn't finish the story!" Princess Cadance said, smiling. "What happened to the unicorn and the princess?"

Prince Shining Armor grinned. "Well, I think the princess was about to reveal her brilliant plan to save them both from the giant."

"Yes," agreed Princess Cadance. "And I think the unicorn was going to do something very brave to get them safely back down the beanstalk."

"Definitely. And I'm pretty sure they fell in love."

"Then what?" asked Princess Cadance. "How does the story end?"

"The same way every good story ends, of course!"

They all lived happily ever after.

The End